GREEDY GRAHAM

KNOW-ALL NANCY

TOO-LATE TOBY

SULKY SUE

TELL-TALE TALLULAH

SICKLY SIMON

BOISTEROUS BILLY

DIRTY DERMOT

RUDE ROGER

SERIOUS SADIE

GROWN-UP GABBY

REVOLTING RONNIE

TV TREVOR

HELPFUL HENRY

TICKLISH TIMMY

CONTRARY CONSTANCE

GREEDY GRAHAM

KNOW-ALL NANCY

FORGETFUL FIONA

IRRITATING IRVING

TELL-TALE TALLULAH

TANTRUM TABITHA

DANGEROUS DAVE

DIRTY DERMOT

RUDE ROGER

PERFECT PRUDENCE

TV TREVOR

BOSSY BETHANY

SILLY SYDNEY

TICKLISH TIMMY

CONTRARY CONSTANCE

WIDE-AWAKE WESLEY

PICKIN' PETER

FORGETFUL FIONA

IRRITATING IRVING

TANTRUM TABITHA

CURIOUS CALVIN

DANGEROUS DAVE

CLUMSY CLARISSA

FRIENDLY FRANCO

PERFECT PRUDENCE

SHY SOPHIE

BOSSY BETHANY

WORRIED WINNIE

SILLY SYDNEY

TOO-LATE TOBY

SULKY SUE

WIDE-AWAKE WESLEY

PICKIN' PETER

SICKLY SIMON

BOISTEROUS BILLY

CURIOUS CALVIN

GROWN-UP GABBY

SERIOUS SADIE

CLUMSY CLARISSA

FRIENDLY FRANCO

To all
'Little Monsters'
everywhere

Published by SPLASH! Publishing Ltd. 1998.
© SPLASH! Holdings Ltd. 1998.
Little Monsters™ is a Trade Mark of SPLASH! Holdings Ltd.
From an original concept by Tony Garth,
written by Heather Pedley, edited by Michael Phipps.
Design and illustration by Ian Jackson and Aileen Raistrick.

ISBN: 1 900207 89 3

little MONSTERS™

CHRISTMAS CAROLE

Written by Heather Pedley - Original Story by Tony Garth
Edited by Michael Phipps

It was the week before Christmas. Everyone was very excited. Christmas trees were being decorated and children everywhere were finishing their letters to Father Christmas. But Winnie had already started to worry. "We don't have a chimney in our house, how will Santa Claus deliver my presents, Dad?" she asked.

"Don't worry," said Winnie's dad. "I'll leave a note for him and ask him to leave your presents in the garden shed!"

Trevor already had a copy of the latest TV guide. "Wow! Look at this… films, quiz shows, specials and, of course, my favourite – cartoons!"

"You'll get square eyes watching all that TV, Trevor," laughed his gran.

"I can't wait for Christmas to come," said Graham. "It's a nonstop feeding frenzy! Just think of all those sweets, all that Christmas pud, chocolates, jelly, ice-cream and good old turkey dinner. Mmmm, yummy!"

"Don't be so greedy, Graham," said his mum.

The next day, during school assembly, the teacher of class one, Miss Harper, gathered all the children together. "Today we are going to learn about the true meaning of Christmas," she said.

"Does this mean we can open our presents now, Miss?" asked Calvin.

"Yeah! Bring on the grub!" said Graham.

"Now, now, quieten down all of you," said Miss Harper. The children fell silent. "So, what is Christmas? What does it mean and why do we celebrate it? We get presents from Santa Claus and we get to eat lots of yummy food!" Miss Harper patted her tummy. "And, if we're really lucky, depending on where we live, we might even get snow. All this is wonderful, but it doesn't tell us anything about the true meaning of Christmas and why we celebrate it, does it?" The children looked at their teacher and then at one another.

Suddenly, Nancy put up her hand. "Yes, Nancy," said Miss Harper. "Do you know something about Christmas?"

Nancy stood up, cleared her throat and gave a little cough. "Ahem! Christmas Day is a birthday. It is a very special time. It is when we celebrate the birth of Jesus, Miss," she said.

"Very good, Nancy," said Miss Harper. "Can you tell me anymore?"

"Yes, Miss, I can," and she walked over to the the model of the nativity. "I think you'll find that baby Jesus was born about 2000 years ago in the town of Bethlehem. In fact, there was no room at the inn, so he was born in a little stable surrounded by animals," said Nancy in her know-it-all voice. "He was sent from heaven to bring peace on earth and goodwill to all men and grew up to be a very special and great man." Nancy looked at all the other children, "Believe me, I know!" she said, rather smugly.

Miss Harper nodded and looked very pleased, "Thank you, Nancy, you are right," she said. "And as part of *our* Christmas celebrations, children, we're going to put on a play. We start rehearsals right away because the performance is – *tomorrow*!" There were gasps of excitement and joy. "Our play will be the Christmas Nativity. It tells the story of the birth of Jesus," continued Miss Harper. "Right, let's hand out the costumes!"

The children were thrilled. "Yeah! All right! Yippee! Hooray!" they all squealed. They had never been in a play before and couldn't wait to get started.

Later that day, Sue was having a big sulk. "I don't want to wear these," she said. "They look silly!"

"All angels have wings," said Mr Franks, the headmaster. "You can't be an angel without wings!"

"Then I *won't* be an angel," Sue replied. "I didn't realise I had to wear silly wings and they're *dirty*!"

As Mr Franks tried to think of a way to cheer Sue up, he turned round and saw Sydney with a towel draped over his face! "Sydney! Try not to be *so* silly. The towel is supposed to be worn like this…" Mr Franks said, turning the towel around. The other shepherds, Irving, Timmy, Peter and Simon had all copied Sydney and were standing in a row with towels draped over their faces, too! Mr Franks tut-tutted as he rearranged the headdresses for them.

"Miss," said Bethany, in her usual bossy tone. "Miss Harper, tell Gabby that *I'm* playing Mary. I'm Jesus' mum!"

"But I want to play the mother," said Gabby. "I'm more grown-up than Bethany."

"But you're the innkeeper's wife. And Roger," said Miss Harper, looking at Roger, "I want you to be very good today because you're playing the role of Joseph, Mary's husband."

"PHRUUPTH!" Roger blew a big raspberry.

"And you can stop that right now!" said Miss Harper, crossly. "Joseph was a very polite man, he didn't go around blowing raspberries!"

"Now, Henry, you're the innkeeper. In the story, Mary and Joseph arrive at the inn and ask if you have a room for the night," said Miss Harper. "Mary is about to have a baby, baby Jesus. You have to tell her that you have no room left at the inn, but they are welcome to stay in the stable where it's warm and dry." Henry was delighted, eager to help Miss Harper in anyway he could.

At last, it was time to start rehearsing. Bethany, dressed as Mary, with Roger, dressed as Joseph, knocked three times on the innkeeper's door.

Henry poked his head out. "Can I help you?" he asked.

"Noooo!" said Roger, rudely, and blew a raspberry.

"Stop that!" said Bethany, sharply. "Yes, you can help us, innkeeper. We have travelled far and I am about to have a baby. Tell me, do you have a room for the night?"

"Why yes, of course," said Henry. "Come on inside, you must be really tired."

"Stop!" cried Mr Franks. "Henry, the inn is full! Tell them they can sleep in the stable." Miss Harper buried her head in her hands.

"It's all right, Sir, we know," said Bethany. "Come on Joseph, let's find the stable," and she dragged Roger off the stage.

"In this part of the story," said Miss Harper, "we have to pretend that Jesus has just been born and that he's sleeping in the manger."

The children gathered around. "But it's just a *doll*, Miss," said Irving.

"I know it's a doll, we're pretending, remember?" explained Miss Harper. "Now, at this point, the three wise men will enter, Nancy, Sadie and... Toby. *Where's* Toby?"

Toby rushed in. "Sorry I'm late, I was putting my costume on."

"Now, the wise men present the gifts... gold, frankincense and myrrh," said Mr Franks.

"But I have a gift, too," said Graham. He handed Mr Franks a tin of peas!

"Peas!" exclaimed Mr Franks, "but why peas?"

"Peas on earth, goodwill to all men," said Graham.

"That's 'peace' Graham, not 'peas', but it's a nice thought. I'm sure Jesus would have liked it."

"Sir, it mentions here holly and ivy," said Calvin, pointing to his song sheet. Who are they?"

"Doh! It's not *who* but *what*!" said Mr Franks. "It's holly as in holly tree and ivy as in, well, ivy," he said, pointing to the wilting ivy plant in the corner.

"Now, as the wise men enter with their gifts, our choir will sing 'Away in a Manger', accompanied by the school band," said Mr Franks. Then he and Miss Harper turned to look at the school band and cringed. It was led by Dave and his friends who were eager to bash their cymbals, tambourines and drums as loud as they could! Mr Franks and Miss Harper quickly plugged their ears with cotton wool!

Mrs Anderson cried, "Are we ready?" and the band and choir started...

It was pandemonium! The music was out of tune and out of time and as for the singing... well!

"Excellent, children! That was, er, different!" said Miss Harper when the din had stopped. "Tomorrow's the big day, so don't forget to be on time and bring your parents with you!" All the children buzzed with excitement as they left the school hall and headed for home that afternoon.

The next day, Mr Franks and Miss Harper were in the staff room drinking tea. In one hour's time, the school hall would be full of parents.

"It's going to be awful, Miss Harper," said Mr Franks, shaking his head.

"I know," agreed Miss Harper, "the rehearsal yesterday was *terrible*! I don't know what we can do! The class will *never* be good enough to perform the play!"

Backstage, the children were busy putting on their costumes. Dave was staring out of the window, dreamily. "I wonder if it'll snow today," he said. "I can't wait to play in the snow on my new sledge."

"Santa is bringing me a doll's house," said Fiona. "At least, I think he is, or, is it a bike, or is it…"

"Constance!" bossed Bethany, "hurry up and put your outfit on, we're running out of time."

"Shan't! Can't! Won't!" replied Constance and walked off.

"I am not amused!" said Sadie – the children were nowhere near ready, they needed help and quick!

Mr Franks had managed to persuade Sue to play an angel in the play but Sue was still sulking about the dirty wings she had to wear. Suddenly, a little voice behind her said, "What's the matter?"

Sue turned around and saw a girl she had never seen before standing there, dressed as an angel. Her wings sparkled and gleamed, her blond hair twinkled and her halo was a shiny gold.

"I won't be an angel because my wings are dirty," said Sue, sulkily.

"But look, Sue, your wings are clean and bright," said the new girl.

Sue smiled when she saw her beautiful wings. "Oh, they're just like yours," she said, happily.

Nancy came over. "Hi. My name's Nancy," she said. "We've never seen you before, are you new here?" she asked.

"Are you Ivy?" asked Calvin, curiously.

"No, I'm Carole, and yes, Nancy, you are right, I am new around her."

"I'm *right*?" Nancy beamed with delight.

"Listen, it looks like you could use some help around here," said Carole.

All the other children wandered over. Dave came away from the window, Trevor looked up from his TV guide and even Graham stopped eating for a second!

Gabby said, "You look so beautiful, Carole. You're just like a real angel. I love your dress."

"Thank you, Gabby," replied Carole.

"How come you know all of our names?" asked Prudence. "Even *I* can't remember everybody's names, and *I'm* perfect!"

"We're *all* perfect," said Carole, smiling.

"What, even me?" asked Dermot.

"Yes, of course," laughed Carole. She picked up the doll that was baby Jesus and handed it to Bethany. "I'll tell you all about Christmas, if you like," said Carole.

"Yes, please!" they all said, and they gathered around.

For the next hour, Carole told them stories about Christmas. She sang them beautiful songs and talked about far away places like Bethlehem and Nazareth. She described the rich and splendid palaces belonging to the three wise men. Carole recited poetry and drew them pictures and maps. The children listened to Carole's stories, and as they did so they felt wonderful. For a while, they forgot all about Santa, presents, TV and food.

Suddenly, Miss Harper burst in. She was surprised to see the children gathered together and didn't notice Carole. "Curtain up in five minutes, everyone," she said. "Are we ready?"

"Yes, Miss," they all replied. Miss Harper smiled before she left.

"Oh, that was wonderful," said Prudence turning to Carole. "Now I really understand what Christmas is about."

"Me, too," said Graham, his eyes were twinkling.

"And me," all the children said, nodding and smiling.

"Well," said Carole, "now it's *your* turn to show everyone how wonderful Christmas is."

"Are you coming with us?" asked Clarissa.

"Yes, yes, do, do," they all begged.

"I'll watch from the side," said Carole.

"You will be here when we've finished, won't you?" asked Dave.

"Yes, I'll always be here. Now, off you go, good luck and be the best that you can."

In the audience, the parents were waiting silently and anxiously. Some of them had cotton wool in their ears, others were quietly groaning! Mrs Anderson started to play the piano as the band and choir took their places. The lights went down and the curtain went up. The nativity began…

Bethany and Roger, dressed as Mary and Joseph, asked the innkeeper if he had a room for the night.

"I'm very sorry," said Henry, the innkeeper. "We're fully booked. But we've a nice comfy stable, full of clean, dry hay." Henry's performance was wonderful.

"Look at yonder star which shines so brightly," said Toby, the wiseman, right on cue.

"We bring you glad tidings of great joy," said Fiona, with a big smile. She had remembered every single word!

Sue's wings glittered, "I am the angel Gabriel," she said. Sue's mum and dad gasped in surprise – for once, their daughter wasn't sulking!

The nativity play was brilliant. The band and choir played and sang perfectly in tune and in time. Mrs Anderson was so surprised that she fell off her chair!

Everybody clapped and cheered. "Encore, more, more," shouted the parents as all the children came to the front of the stage to take a bow. The nativity was a huge success and Miss Harper and Mr Franks, who were both shocked and surprised, were patted on the back and congratulated. The children were thrilled. They all rushed backstage to see Carole, but they couldn't find her.

"Miss Harper, have you seen Carole anywhere?" asked Sadie.

"*Carole*?" replied Miss Harper. "I'm afraid I don't know a girl called Carole."

"Yes you do," said Nancy. "She's the new girl in our class."

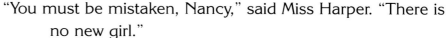

"You must be mistaken, Nancy," said Miss Harper. "There is no new girl."

"But there is," said Dave, "and it's thanks to her that our play was such a success."

"Dave's right," said Sue. "Carole taught us the true meaning of Christmas."

Miss Harper just smiled and shook her head. "Well I'm pleased that you all now understand what Christmas is *really* about. You can have fun with your presents, watch lots of TV, eat fabulous food and play in the snow, but Christmas is about being *together*. It's about sharing, friendship and goodwill to *everyone*."

"We know," said the children together. They were *all* very happy.

Mr Franks came over and said, "Today class, you were as good as gold, you were wonderful, and if this girl called Carole helped to make that happen, then she really *does* know the true meaning of Christmas."

Everybody nodded and smiled. They all understood. "We know," said Sadie, grinning from ear to ear, "she's a very special *Christmas Carole*."

Outside the school, everything had turned white! Everywhere you looked, there was a thick blanket of snow. Lights twinkled, presents were being placed under richly decorated trees and you could hear the sounds of laughter and happiness in all the tiny houses.

High up in the sky, a little girl called Carole, whose wings sparkled and gleamed, hovered above the school. As promised, she had seen all of the nativity play and was very proud of the children from class one. She knew her job was done. As she flew homewards, she looked back towards the school. "Happy Christmas, everyone," she called, and then was gone. All that was left was a trail of sparkling gold fluttering in the snow.

The End

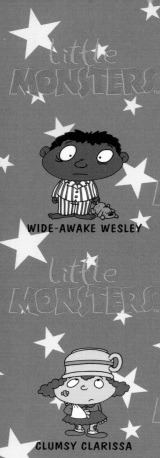

SILLY SYDNEY

TICKLISH TIMMY

CONTRARY CONSTANCE

WIDE-AWAKE WESLEY

PICKIN' PETER

FORGETFUL FIONA

IRRITATING IRVING

TANTRUM TABITHA

CURIOUS CALVIN

DANGEROUS DAVE

CLUMSY CLARISSA

FRIENDLY FRANCO

PERFECT PRUDENCE

SHY SOPHIE

BOSSY BETHANY

WORRIED WINNIE

SILLY SYDNEY

TOO-LATE TOBY

SULKY SUE

WIDE-AWAKE WESLEY

PICKIN' PETER

SICKLY SIMON

BOISTEROUS BILLY

CURIOUS CALVIN

GROWN-UP GABBY

SERIOUS SADIE

CLUMSY CLARISSA

FRIENDLY FRANCO